STRONGHOLD

SUPER HUMAN

STRONGHOLD

R. T. MARTIN

darbycreek

MINNEAPOLIS

Darby Creek
A division of Lerner Publishing Group, Inc.
241 First Avenue North
Minneapolis, MN 55401 USA

For reading levels and more information, look up this title at www.lernerbooks.com.

The images in this book are used with the permission of: iStock.com/Vladimirovic; iStock.com/edge69; Igartist 79/Shutterstock.com; iStock.com/sinemaslow.

Main body text set in Janson Text LT Std 12/17.5.
Typeface provided by Adobe Systems.

Library of Congress Cataloging-in-Publication Data

Names: Martin, R. T., 1988- author.
  Title: Stronghold / R.T. Martin.
  Description: Minneapolis : Darby Creek, 2018. | Series: Superhuman | Summary:
    On her sixthteenth birthday, Aisha is shocked to discover she has somehow
    acquired superhuman strength, an ability she wants to keep secret at all
    costs, but when an earthquake ravages her school Aisha must choose between
    protecting her secret or using her strength to save her friends from
    certain death.
  Identifiers: LCCN 2017016314 (print) | LCCN 2017029972 (ebook) | ISBN
    9781512498370 (eb pdf) | ISBN 9781512498301 (lb : alk. paper) | ISBN
    9781541510524 (pb : alk. paper)
  Subjects: | CYAC: Friendship—Fiction. | Secrets—Fiction. | Muscle
    strength—Fiction. | High schools—Fiction. | Schools—Fiction.
  Classification: LCC PZ7.1.M37346 (ebook) | LCC PZ7.1.M37346 St 2018 (print) |
    DDC [Fic]—dc23
  LC record available at https://lccn.loc.gov/2017016314

Manufactured in the United States of America
1-43581-33362-7/6/2017

For Maria

SIXTEEN YEARS AGO, ON APRIL 12, SIX PEOPLE FROM AROUND THE COUNTRY WERE BORN WITH A HIDDEN SPECIAL ABILITY.

On their sixteenth birthday, they each develop their special ability for the first time. Whether they can soar through the clouds, run faster than the speed of light, or tear through a brick wall, all the teenagers must choose how to use their powers. Will they keep their abilities secret? Will they use them only to benefit themselves? Or will they attempt to help others—even if the risks are greater than they could imagine? One way or another, each teen will have to learn what it means to be . . . superhuman.

1

Happy birthday to me, happy birthday to me,
Aisha sang to herself in her head. She knew
no one would sing for her here. No one even
knew it was her sixteenth birthday. It was only
her second week at this school and she hadn't
made any friends yet.

Sitting in class, she may as well have
been invisible. No one even looked at her. At
her old school, she may have been passing
sketches or notes to one of her friends, but
now they were hundreds of miles away,
and she had to make a new life here in
this tiny town of Bloomington, a far cry
from Chicago.

The history teacher was explaining why it had been a bad idea for the United States to enter Vietnam while Aisha twirled her pencil and thought about how much better her birthday would have been back home. There would have been a party. She would have gotten well-wishes and hugs at school. It would have been fun. Her friends in Chicago made a huge deal out of their sixteenth birthdays, celebrating with incredible parties. Aisha had planned to do that too, but the move spoiled those plans. She lived too far away for any of her old friends to come visit, and who here would come to a party for a girl they didn't know?

Several of her friends from home had sent her celebratory text messages or posted on her social media this morning, but it wasn't the same.

The bell rang. "All right, that's it for today," the teacher said. "Remember to read chapter twenty-two for tomorrow."

Aisha got up from her desk and grabbed her bag. So far she wasn't doing any extracurricular activities—no sports, no clubs. There was only one that she was even mildly interested in—the school's newspaper. She'd been a writer for the one at her old school, and she couldn't help being interested in the one here as well.

On her second day, she'd picked up the *Bloomington High Herald* and read through it. It wasn't bad, but the stories weren't nearly as interesting as they'd been in Chicago. Also there was a typo in the sports section . . . unless the volleyball team really had won by five *pants*.

At her last school, she had covered sports. Even though she wasn't very athletic, she had enjoyed the reporting process, and it was cool to see her writing distributed to the whole school and posted online. Last week, Aisha had asked a teacher about joining the newspaper's staff. She had even filled out the registration form, but she wasn't sure if she would actually go. Today, she was even less sure. Starting at a new school was stressful enough without adding a new activity.

At her locker, Aisha stashed the books and folders she wouldn't need that night while grabbing the ones she would. *I could just go home*, she thought. *I don't have to join the paper.*

She closed her locker. *No. Avoiding clubs and sports isn't going to get me any friends, and I* need *to make some friends or life here is going to be horrible until I graduate.*

The paper's office was located in the basement of the school. Aisha chewed her lip and stared down the hall toward the doors that led outside. Squaring her shoulders and taking a deep breath, she headed down the stairs instead.

It took her a while to find the room. The basement was a maze of winding hallways. She reached three dead ends before she found the office tucked away across from a custodian's closet. She was surprised there was anything down here, much less the school paper.

There were already about a dozen other students in the room by the time she got there. A teacher sat at the front behind a desk cluttered with paper. There didn't seem to be any organization. It was as if whenever anyone tossed a handwritten or typed article on the desk, the teacher just left it wherever it had landed. Most of the kids were chattering away or hunched over notebooks and computers. It was definitely a smaller operation than the newsroom she'd worked in back home.

"Excuse me," Aisha said to the teacher. "I'd like to join the newspaper. I just registered for it." She held out the form to him.

"What? It's April." He was giving her a confused look over the top of thick glasses.

"I'm new here." Aisha could feel her face flushing. "I just started a couple of weeks ago"

"Ah," he said, taking the form. "In that case, I'm Mr. Westlake. Why don't you take a seat, and we'll find a group for you in just a little bit."

Aisha took a seat next to a girl in the back row and pulled out a notebook and pencil from her backpack. The girl next to her didn't even look up from her cell phone.

"Okay," Mr. Westlake said, getting up from his chair, "let's get started." The room quieted as the students took their seats or shifted to face forward. "First, I want to talk about the last issue. There was a typo in sports. That's not okay, people. Make sure you proofread your articles before they go to print. Second, I'm still waiting on that interview with the principal." He seemed to be addressing four kids sitting around a computer by the door. "She said you haven't even spoken to her yet. Get on that now."

He paused, then turned back to the students. "I wasn't kidding. Get on that right now. Go down to her office. Go, go, go." The group quickly gathered their things and headed out of the room. Aisha swallowed heavily as she watched the kids scramble. She wiped her sweaty palms on her pants. Maybe this was a mistake. Not only was she anxious about being here in the first place, but the way this teacher was so comfortable with calling out students made her squirm in her seat. Aisha considered slipping out now and began fiddling with her pencil, a constant nervous habit.

Mr. Westlake was just beginning to talk to the sports reporters, another group of four

clustered around a small table, when—*crack*—
the pencil snapped in her hand. She flinched
as half of the pencil flew past her face. The
girl next to her looked over in surprise and
gave a sympathetic little smile. Aisha grabbed
another pencil out of her bag and started
tapping it this time.

Crack. The second pencil snapped. This
time, the girl next to her chuckled. Aisha
grabbed a third pencil. *Crack.* Once again, the
pencil snapped. Now the girl next to her was
actually stifling full-blown laughter.

"What's going on back there?" Mr.
Westlake asked, noticing the commotion.

"Nothing," Aisha said. "Nothing, I just—I
broke my pencil. Sorry."

"Well, try to keep it down," Mr. Westlake
said. His expression softened and he gave a
teasing smile. "You can break pencils on your
own time."

The other students chuckled. Aisha could
feel her face turning red as she hastily grabbed
a pen out of her bag—she'd just broken her
last pencil. The girl next to her was still

suppressing her laughter.

Great, now everyone thinks I'm the weird pencil-breaking girl, Aisha thought, desperately trying to avoid eye contact with the girl. *I should've just gone home.*

After sending the sports team on their way, Mr. Westlake turned back to Aisha. "All right, what's your name again?"

"Aisha."

"Well, Aisha, we've got to find a group for you. Have you worked on a school paper before?"

She nodded.

"She can be in our group," the girl next to her said. "We're down a person anyway."

"Great. You'll be on local news, Aisha," Mr. Westlake confirmed.

"I'm Ella," the girl next to her said almost immediately. She didn't even wait for a response from Aisha before she gestured for two other students to come over. One of them was short and wore glasses. The other one . . . looked exactly like Ella with a slightly shorter haircut. "This," she gestured toward the shorter kid, "is

Cal, and this is Ben. He's my—"

"Twin brother," Ben finished.

"I'm Aisha," she said. She wanted to say more but couldn't find any words.

"We do local news," Ella said, "so we cover stuff like—"

"Grand openings, events in town, and, occasionally, some local politics stuff." Ben seamlessly picked up the sentence. "I wanted to do sports, but Mr. Westlake gave that to Kyle's group because he's on the basketball team, so sometimes he's got inside info."

Aisha was just about to tell him that she'd written about sports at her last school, but she was cut off. "Okay, local news group," Mr. Westlake said. "The corn maze is starting next week, which means the city will be setting it up over the next few days. I want you guys on that. Aisha, Ella, Ben, Tim." Aisha looked around. *Tim? I thought his name was Cal?*

"Two of you should cover the corn maze. I want the other two to work on the article about fracking in the area."

Fracking? Aisha thought. She'd heard about fracking before. It was a way of mining natural gas from slate hundreds of feet below the ground. In Chicago, fracking had seemed like one of those far away things that people only read about. Apparently, it was going on right in Bloomington's backyard.

"And start coming up with other article ideas for future issues," Mr. Westlake continued. "There's always something happening here."

Doubt it, Aisha thought.

"You're the ones that need to know about it," Mr. Westlake finished. "All right, get going." He sat back down at his desk and started rifling through the mess of papers.

As the others pulled their chairs closer, Aisha turned to Cal. "Did he call you Tim?"

Cal rolled his eyes. "Yeah, that's my real name. I won a state math competition in sixth grade and Ella and Ben started calling me Calculus."

"Yeah, we did," Ben said, putting up a hand to high-five Ella. She did not return the gesture.

"Eventually it got shortened to Cal, and," he shrugged, "I don't know. It just kind of stuck. Occasionally teachers call me Tim because that's what's on their attendance sheets."

Aisha laughed. "Okay, I guess I'll call you Cal then?"

"Most people do," he said cheerfully.

"We'll cover the corn maze," Ella said to Aisha. "It's an easy story, we can—"

"Just use a bunch of the text from last year," Ben said.

"Yeah," Ella said. "It's the same basic story. We'll just plug in some of the new stuff and move things around a bit."

"Ben and I will try to find out more about that sinkhole out in Lanesfield," Cal said. Aisha gave him a confused look. "There have been some sinkholes in the last year or two. People think it's because of the fracking." Aisha still looked confused. "Lanesfield is the next town over."

Aisha nodded, finally up to speed. "Got it."

Ella told her that she wouldn't have to worry about anything today. Ella would dig up the old corn maze article, and they'd start working on the new one tomorrow. For the next hour, Ella, Cal, and Ben explained the ins and outs of working at the paper—when things were due, what they'd written about in the last few editions, and the kinds of stories that Mr. Westlake liked. By the time they were done, Aisha was feeling good, much better than she had been before. She leaned down to pick up her bag when—*thrap*—the strap ripped out of its seam. She grabbed the other one—*thrap*.

Her group watched this happen and paused for a moment before all bursting into laughter. Aisha was mortified. Things had been going so well. Why was everything breaking?

"Nice work, Aish—" Ella paused, "No wait, we're going to call you Muscles."

Aisha grinned and shook her head, feeling relieved to find a group she at least felt comfortable hanging around with. *And*, she figured, *there are worse nicknames*.

"Welcome to the club," Cal said.

2

The high school was two miles from the apartment building where Aisha lived with her father. She biked home past little shops, houses, a park, and a junkyard that smelled like garbage. They'd moved to Oklahoma after her dad lost his job. A friend of his had offered him a new one here in Bloomington. Without any other options, they had packed up and moved.

At the time, Aisha had been angry. She'd wanted to stay in the city she knew with the friends she already had, but the decision was out of her hands. She'd calmed down after a while when she realized that her father hadn't wanted to move either. He was leaving his old life too. Now they just had each other in this unfamiliar town.

The apartment was small. Aisha's dad had started the new job right away, so they'd moved into the first apartment that was available. But for the past few weeks he had been trying to find something a little bigger.

Aisha sat down in the living room and turned on the TV. She usually tried to get her homework out of the way as soon as she came home from school, but she figured if this was her only way of celebrating her sixteenth birthday, she'd let it go for the day.

Later that evening, her father burst through the door and tossed a handful of confetti into the air, which Aisha realized upon closer inspection was actually tiny scraps of colored office paper.

"There's the birthday girl!" he said. "How was your day?"

Aisha shrugged. "Fine, I guess."

"Just fine?" He sat down next to her on the couch. "Well, in that case, I've got a surprise for you."

Aisha looked at him and raised her eyebrows.

"I asked my boss what the nicest restaurant in town is, and we're going there tonight. It's some place called Prestige—very fancy."

"I don't want to get dressed up," she said.

"Then don't!" her father said excitedly. "It's your birthday. You can do whatever you want! You can wear a bathrobe there if you like!"

Aisha smiled. Maybe she would do just that. "I should get my homework done now if we're going out tonight."

"Good plan," he said. "Do you need anything in the meantime—soda, a snack? I'll run right out and grab it."

"I'm okay, but thank you." He always made a big deal out of her birthday. *And he's being extra nice this year because of the move*, Aisha figured.

She did her homework until seven, when her dad came out of his room wearing his best three-piece suit. Aisha's jaw dropped. Apparently he wasn't kidding about the fancy dinner. "You may not be getting dressed up," he said, "but I'm going to make my daughter's birthday as special as I can. Shall we?"

Aisha couldn't help but grin. "We shall."

His boss had been right. Prestige was incredibly fancy. The tables all had white tablecloths and candles on them. There were multiple forks and spoons at the place settings. The waiters all wore matching suits, and everyone but Aisha was dressed up like they were headed to the opera. She didn't feel out of place in her skinny jeans and old sweater though. Like her dad said, it was her birthday and she could wear whatever she wanted.

While they waited for their food, Aisha told her dad about the school newspaper and the people she'd met. He told her funny stories about some of his new coworkers. For a while, things didn't seem so bad here. She had her dad. There were kids at her school that she liked and who seemed to like her. And she was pretty sure she would enjoy working on the school paper, even if it was different from what she was used to.

The waiter gently placed her entrée in front of her, a stuffed chicken dish. She picked up her fork, but when she moved it toward her food, she noticed that the fork had bent at a ninety-degree angle. She held it in front of her in surprise.

"Whoa," her father said. "How did that happen?"

"I don't know," she said. "I just picked it up, and it bent."

Her father flagged down a waiter. "My daughter needs a new fork."

The waiter took the fork from Aisha and examined it with a confused look on his face. "Ah . . . yes, right away, miss," he said with a little bow.

He left for a moment and returned with a new fork. Aisha started eating while her father made jokes about how strong she was getting. She glanced over and saw their waiter standing near the kitchen. He was showing the fork to a group of coworkers, whispering and pointing at Aisha. She sunk a little in her chair and felt her face go red again.

Her dad noticed right away. "Don't worry, honey. It's just a fork." He looked around the restaurant. "That guy probably had it before you." He pointed to a man sitting a few tables over. That guy was so stuffed with muscles that his suit coat looked like it was about to burst off his torso. Aisha laughed and felt better. Still . . . it was odd. She'd had a real streak of breaking things today.

3

Beep—Beep—BANG—Clank—Clatter—Clang!

All she had tried to do was shut off her alarm, but when she hit the snooze button, the thing burst into dozens of tiny pieces. Aisha barely had time to process what just happened before there was anxious knocking at her door.

"What happened? Are you okay?" her father asked.

"I'm fine," she said quickly. "I—I—I knocked my alarm clock off the nightstand." In truth it looked like she'd hit the clock with a sledgehammer. "I'm fine though, really."

"Okay," her father said. "Breakfast is ready when you are."

Aisha got out of bed and looked at the pieces of the clock. She tried to pick up a piece of the shattered plastic, but it broke again as soon as she touched it. She tried once more, but the next piece broke too. *I can't touch anything*, she thought. Her breath quickened as she felt a panicked tightness in her chest.

What's happening to me? Sitting back down on her bed, she tried to calm down. She focused on her breathing until it returned to normal. It must have taken longer than she thought because her dad asked if she was all right again.

"Yeah," she said, "just getting dressed." She put on her clothes and turned to head out of her room. When she grabbed the door knob, she felt it crumple in her grip. The door was open, but the knob had a perfect indentation of her hand. *No, no, no, this can't be happening.*

Her father had laid out a bowl of cereal and some fruit for her. He was sitting at the table, sipping coffee while scrolling through the online news on his phone. Aisha carefully pulled out the chair across from him and sat down. She paused for a moment before picking up the spoon to eat her cereal. She got the spoon into the cereal, but when she shifted her grip to lift it back up, it bent just like the fork had at the restaurant. All the cereal spilled back into the bowl. Just before her dad looked up from his phone to talk to her, she stuffed the bent spoon into a pocket so that he wouldn't see it.

"Are you going to go to the school paper again today?"

She'd completely forgotten about that. "Yeah," she said as a reflex. "I think so."

"Good," he said, taking a bite of his toast. "I know things are hard right now, but give it time. Eventually, you may find that you actually like it here." He gave her a little half smile. "You're not eating."

"I'm not really hungry this morning." That was a lie. She was starving, but the last thing she wanted to do was bend another utensil in front of her father. "I think I'm still full from all the food at dinner last night."

He got up and grabbed a small bag of chips

from one of the cabinets. "Here, take this in case you get hungry before lunch." He tossed the bag to her. She grabbed it out of the air and it popped, shooting chips all over the place. Her dad's eyes widened.

"Thanks," she said without acknowledging what had just happened. She rolled the top of the bag down to keep the rest of the chips inside. Standing up, she added casually, "I should get going."

"You've still got a few minutes before—"

"I have to go," she cut him off, grabbed her bag and rushed out the door, making sure to barely touch the knob. "Love you," she said just before it closed.

Once outside the apartment building, Aisha was about to unlock her bike and ride it to school when she thought, *I'd better not. I don't want to break that too*. She walked the two miles instead. Normally, she would have made it to school with plenty of time to spare, but today she was cutting it close.

She rushed to her locker out of breath and desperately hoping she wouldn't be late to her first class. She tried to enter the lock combo, but the dial crushed under her grip and ripped straight out of the metal door.

It was the last straw. Aisha was close to tears now. Frustrated and confused, she stared at the broken dial in her hand as the bell rang. Now she was late too. *What is happening to me? What am I supposed to do? I can't touch anything without destroying it!*

"Something wrong with your locker?" It was the school custodian. Aisha didn't say anything. She just held her hand out and showed him the crushed dial. He took it, gave it a puzzled look, and said, "This is a new one to me." He put it in his pocket, pulled out a screwdriver from his tool belt, and jammed it where the dial should have been. After he wiggled it around a bit, the locker popped open.

"Thank you," Aisha said, grabbing some of her books.

"No problem. I'll see about getting a new lock on there." He paused. Aisha must still have looked like she was on the verge of tears.

"And don't worry about this—sometimes things break," he said with a shrug.

She thanked him again and rushed to her biology class. Her teacher had already begun writing notes on the whiteboard when she walked into the room. "My locker broke," Aisha explained. "I couldn't get it open." The teacher waved away the excuse and continued the lecture.

Aisha sat down and opened her notebook. She reached into her bag, about to grab a pencil, but stopped herself. She found a pen instead, but when she gripped it, she heard a snap and felt liquid running through her fingers. When she took her hand out of her bag, it was covered in blue ink. The notebooks and textbooks in her bag were probably coated as well.

Great, she thought. *So taking notes is out of the question. I'll just make sure to pay close attention.* She tried to focus as hard as she could, but it was no use. She couldn't stop wondering what was happening to her. The question ran through her mind over and over again.

She couldn't take notes in any of her classes. She couldn't focus either. In the bathroom, she had tried to wash the ink off, but it barely helped. Her hand looked like she'd been crushing blueberries all day. Eating lunch was a mess too. It was especially difficult to get the chips one by one from the bag to her mouth—they kept crumbling. Eventually she just poured them out of the bag directly into her mouth.

When the final bell rang at the end of the day, Aisha couldn't have been more relieved. *I made it*, she thought as she gathered her things and headed to her locker. *I've never wanted to go home so badly in my life.*

She was putting some ink-covered books back in her locker when she heard, "Muscles! I've got the old corn maze article." It was Ella. "Let's head downstairs and—what happened to your locker?"

"It broke," Aisha said, closing the door and realizing that she'd completely forgotten about the school paper. "Sorry, Ella, I think I'm just going to go home today."

"Oh no you're not," she said. "I'm not doing this whole article by myself. Come on, let's go downstairs."

Aisha was too exhausted to argue, so she followed Ella down to the paper's office. Cal and Ben were already there, sitting at one of the computers.

"Hey, Muscles," Ben said when he saw her. "Ready for your first article?"

"I guess so," she replied.

Ella was right—the article would be easy. The corn maze was an annual event that didn't change much, so the text from last year was mostly still accurate. Ella filled her in on some of the changes to this year's maze and they started writing.

"Read it over and add some bullet points that you want to make sure we mention. I'll do the same," Ella said.

"Uhh—I probably shouldn't," Aisha said. Breaking a computer would be much worse than breaking a pen. She hastily tried to think of a reasonable excuse. "Computers . . . hurt my eyes."

"But didn't you say you worked for your last school's paper?" Ella said, now clearly suspicious. "Didn't you use a computer then?"

"No," Aisha lied again. "They used . . . uhh, they used tablets. With adjustable blue light settings. Easier on the eyes."

"Fancy," said Cal. She couldn't tell if he was buying it or not.

Even though Ella kept giving Aisha suspicious glances, the others let the issue go. Aisha didn't have to use a computer. Instead she dictated what she wanted to write, and Ella typed up the bullet points.

This isn't working, Aisha thought. *Something is wrong with me and I need to figure out what it is.* A scene played out in her mind, a scene in which everyone discovered what was happening to her and she became an outcast. She and her father would be forced to move to a new place, and the same thing would probably happen there.

Aisha felt her heart sink as she thought, *My life is over.*

4

Aisha was able to hold it together as she and Ella worked on the article, but when she walked home, tears started streaming down her face. *People will think I'm a freak. I won't be able to go to school. I won't have any friends. Bloomington will never seem like home. Maybe I'll never feel at home anywhere in the world.* The tears wouldn't stop coming, and she couldn't slow down her mind.

The walk home felt like it took forever. But Aisha was walking slowly because she didn't really want to get home. Her dad would probably have questions for her, and she didn't want to confront that. He had known something was off this morning. And now she realized that when he left for work, he would have seen her bike still chained to the rack outside their apartment. She'd have to come up with an excuse for why she hadn't taken it.

The smell hit her before she realized where she was. That garbage smell—old, rotting wood mixed with dirt and mold. She was near the junkyard. She was about to keep walking when something caught her eye—a broken down washing machine. The entire junkyard was filled with piles of cabinets, appliances, and cars. Tons of large, broken items that wouldn't be missed if they were broken even more.

Maybe I could practice here, she thought. *Maybe I can teach myself to pick something up without breaking it.*

The gate to the chain-link fence was unlocked, and Aisha stepped inside. As she wandered through, it seemed like no one else was around.

Aisha went deep into the junkyard—less of a chance that someone would see her if they entered without her hearing or seeing them first. She put her bag by an old, broken stove and found a pile of discarded wood and metal. It was disgusting—the wood rotting and rain damaged, and the metal nearly rusted through, but this would be perfect for practice.

Mornings in mid-April here were still somewhat chilly, so Aisha kept a pair of spare gloves in her backpack. She hastily pulled them on to protect her hands before bending down. She tried to pick up a tall stake of wood that looked like it had been part of a fence at some point, but the moment she gripped it, it snapped in half. Aisha felt the tears of frustration starting to come again, but she shook off the feeling and took a deep breath. *That was just my first try*, she thought. *I can do this.*

She found another piece of wood. This time, she grabbed the edge of it very gently. Sliding the wood out of the pile, she focused all her energy on not gripping too tightly. She got it out of the pile, but when she tried to lift it up, it snapped.

Aisha let out a deep sigh. Maybe metal won't break. Very carefully, she picked up a metal rod, but after only a few moments in her grasp, it bent and broke in half. She looked for a piece that would be stronger and found a thick pipe. Once again, she picked it up. This time, she was able to hold it without it breaking. She let out a sigh of relief.

She let the pipe fall out of her hand. *Let's see if I can hold something smaller.*

For the next few hours, Aisha picked up various pieces of scrap. For a while, everything she touched broke, but after some practice, she was able to hold the metal objects without bending or breaking them. Once she had that down, she moved on to larger pieces of wood, then smaller pieces. Once she was able to hold them, she experimented with varying levels of pressure. How much could she apply without the pieces snapping? The answer was not a lot, but she was learning her limits.

The sun was nearly down when she finally thought to herself, *As long as I'm extra careful, I should be able to make it through tomorrow.* She grabbed her bag and headed toward the junkyard's entrance to go home.

It's going to be fine, she thought. *I just need to come up with an excuse for why I didn't take my bike this morning, and I'll be all set.* She made a left around a pile of rusty appliances and stopped dead in her tracks. Ella was standing there.

She had a smirk on her face as she said, "You're having a *really* interesting day, huh?"

5

"I—I—I was just—"

Ella put up a hand. "You were just bending and snapping pieces of metal like they were twigs. I saw."

"You followed me?" Aisha asked, her mind still trying to process that Ella had just seen everything.

Ella nodded. "You can't act as weird as you did today and expect me not to follow you. I *am* a journalist, you know." She gestured toward all the broken pieces of scrap that Aisha had left behind. "How long has that been going on?"

"Those are—this isn't—they're mostly rotted through, so—" Aisha was having trouble coming up with an excuse. "Since yesterday," she finally spat out, giving up.

"Uh huh." Ella pulled out a small notepad and a pen. "How are you able to do it?"

"I don't know." She pointed at the notepad. "What's that for?"

"I report local news. This seems newsworthy."

Aisha took a step forward, pulled the pad from Ella's grasp, and ripped it in half with incredible ease.

Ella pointed at the pieces of the notepad. "I had other notes in there, you know."

Aisha looked down at the pieces in her hand. In the heat of the moment, tearing up the notepad had seemed like the right thing to do, but now she just felt like she'd been overly dramatic. "Oh, uh . . . sorry." She handed the remains of the notepad to Ella.

Ella shook her head and stuffed the scraps into her bag. "So how are you able to do all that?"

"I don't know," Aisha said quickly, glancing around to make sure no one else was close enough to hear her. "It just—it just happened. I don't know why."

"You didn't get hit by an asteroid or fall in chemical waste or anything yesterday?"

Aisha flexed her hands in stress. "Would you keep your voice down?" she hissed. Ella arched her eyebrows as if to point out that Aisha still hadn't answered the question. "It was my birthday, I guess, but nothing—nothing special happened."

Ella's face lit up a bit. "Happy birthday! You didn't say anything."

"Yeah, well, I was a little distracted." Ella was still smiling, which made Aisha smile too, despite her fears about Ella's discovery. She felt herself relax a bit. "But thanks. Listen, I don't want anyone to know about—" She pointed back toward the pieces of scrap. "About this. Please, I'm begging you not to tell anyone. Even I don't understand what's happening to me."

Ella scrunched up her face for a bit and then said, "Okay."

"Okay?"

"Yeah, I won't tell anyone. It seems like things are hard enough for you right now."

"Thanks," Aisha said. "I appreciate it."

The girls walked together toward the entrance of the junkyard in silence. Once they were out, Ella turned to head left, and Aisha turned right. Before walking away, Ella said, "I'll see you tomorrow at the paper. We still need to polish up the corn maze article."

"Okay," Aisha said. "I'll see you tomorrow."

Ella started walking down the sidewalk but shouted over her shoulder, "You owe me a notepad!"

Aisha walked the rest of the way home thinking about what had just happened. The fear that Ella would tell everyone what she knew wasn't completely gone, but what was done was done.

Her father was cooking in the kitchen when she got home. "You're back late," he said.

"I was working at the paper," she answered. "It took a little longer than I thought it would."

"You didn't take your bike today."

"It was really nice out this morning," she said as she sat at the table. "I thought it would be good to walk."

"Ah," he said, "so that's why you left early."

With dinner ready, they sat down together to eat. Her dad asked her about school and told her he picked up a new backpack, pencils, and alarm clock for her.

"Thanks," Aisha said, keeping her gaze on her plate. "The past few days have been a little . . . weird."

"Yeah, what happened to your doorknob? It looks like it was crushed or something."

Aisha felt her whole body tense up. "You never noticed that before? It was like that when we moved in," she lied. "I think it's supposed to fit your hand. It fits mine perfectly." She tried to change the subject. "I'm also gonna need a couple of small notepads for the paper. Everyone has them but me. They're good for taking notes."

He nodded. "I'll get some of those tomorrow." He took a bite of his food and chewed thoughtfully. "I can't believe I hadn't noticed that about the doorknob. I swear it felt normal to me before."

It was hard to eat dinner. Aisha had to hold the utensils very carefully. Although her father seemed to notice she was acting strange, he didn't say anything about it, and Aisha was grateful for that. When she was done, she went to her room to do her homework.

Her assignments were a good distraction for a while, but the moment she finished her mind started racing again. *Ella could write about what I can do in the paper. What if everyone finds out? I could deny everything, but that custodian knows I broke my locker.* She could feel her limbs go numb as the panic spread throughout her body. *Should I tell Dad? No, Ella knows and that's already too many people.* She took a deep breath and counted to ten. After ten, she felt a little better. *What's done is done,* she reminded herself. *I'll have to trust that Ella will keep the secret.*

6

"She's losing her mind," Aisha's English teacher said.

Aisha practically snapped her pen when she heard that comment. She'd been trying to carefully take notes all day, but she had to hold the pen so delicately that it looked like a first-grader had written them. Any amount of pressure she applied would cause the pen to snap. She'd broken one this morning but had made it through the rest of the day without further incident.

"By act four, she's completely lost it." The teacher was describing a character in the Shakespeare play they were reading, but today's lecture was hitting a little too close to home for Aisha. She hadn't seen Ella all day, and the idea that her secret might have been revealed was driving *her* out of her mind.

History was just as bad for Aisha, and she couldn't pay attention for most of the period. At her locker, which was still broken, she half expected Ella to come find her, but she didn't. Once again, Aisha was tempted to just go home, but she forced herself to go to the meeting for the paper. She reminded herself that she couldn't live in fear for the rest of her life.

She made her way down the stairs and through the winding hallways. In the newspaper office, kids were hunched over notebooks and computers speaking quietly to one another as usual. She saw her group in the corner. Ella was leaning back in a chair with her feet up on a desk.

"I'm going to find out eventually," Ben said.

"Well, you won't find out from me," Ella said with a smirk.

"Find out what?" Aisha asked.

Ben turned to face her. "Ella knows something, and she's not telling me what it is."

"How do you know I'm—"

"Not telling me something?" Ben finished for her. "I'm your twin. I can tell."

"What are you guys working on?" Aisha asked Cal, desperate to change the subject.

"We're still writing about the fracking," Cal said. "The company that does it wouldn't give us an interview. I called their one-eight-hundred number and spent forty-five minutes on the phone before getting transferred to someone's assistant who said that they wouldn't answer my questions."

"That's interesting," Aisha said, pretending to be excited.

Cal snorted. "Not really."

"We should probably get to work on the corn maze stuff, right?" she said to Ella then, still trying to change the subject.

Ella gave a little laugh. "Yeah, we should. We can work on that computer over there." She stood up. "I'll type," she said, looking straight at Aisha.

"I'm going to find out," Ben said as they walked away. "You can't keep secrets from me."

The girls walked to the computer on the other side of the room. Ella sat in the chair right in front of it, and Aisha pulled one up next to her.

"So you didn't tell him anything?" Aisha asked in a hushed voice.

"I can neither confirm nor deny that I even have a secret to tell," Ella said and winked at her.

Aisha smiled and felt a whole day of pent-up stress leave her body. "Thanks."

"I think we should talk about the carousel before the cook-off section since it's new," Ella said, pointing to the article on the screen.

"Good idea."

By four thirty, they had finished the article. It was actually pretty good too. When they turned it in to Mr. Westlake, he glanced over it and gave them a thumbs-up. "Start thinking of ideas for your next article," he said. "I'll expect you to have at least one by tomorrow."

The girls left while Ben and Cal continued working on their piece. They went up the stairs, but just as Aisha turned to head for the front door, Ella grabbed her arm and said, "Wait. We're going this way."

Ella led Aisha to a part of the school she hadn't been to before—a room behind the gymnasium. It was the weight room. They stepped inside, and Ella headed straight for the barbells. "Come over here," she said.

Aisha paused, glancing over her shoulder. "Isn't some team going to come in here any second now?"

"No," Ella said. "The only team that uses it this time of year is the baseball team, and they're at an away game right now." She motioned for Aisha to step out of the doorway. "Come on."

Aisha walked over hesitantly. "What do you want me to do?"

Ella pointed at some one-handed, fifty-pound weights sitting on a rack in front of a wall-to-wall mirror. "Pick those up."

Aisha stepped forward and stared at the weights with uncertainty. She glanced over at

Ella once more, who nodded encouragingly. Aisha lifted a weight in each hand as if they weighed nothing at all. They were as light as a pencil had been a week ago. She couldn't help but laugh at how easy it was.

"Not bad," Ella said as Aisha put the weights back where they belonged. "Let's see just how much you can do. Put a couple of those hundred pounders on that barbell."

Aisha grabbed two one-hundred-pound weights from a stack on the floor. She put them on the barbell, and then lifted it easily over her head. She laughed again. *Well, this is pretty awesome!* she thought. The barbell was so light that she started holding the whole thing with one hand, then twirling it around like a baton.

"All right, let's crank it up a notch," Ella said.

Aisha grabbed a couple more hundred-pound weights and added them to the barbell. It weighed six hundred pounds now. She bent down and grabbed the bar with both hands, still expecting it to be heavy. This time it was, but not as heavy as it should have felt. It felt more like she was lifting a box filled with books.

"Okay, this is kind of cool," she said with a shy smile, looking over at Ella. But it was clear the other girl wasn't listening. She was just staring with her mouth slightly open.

After a moment, Ella shook off the awed expression. "Let's keep going, Muscles."

Aisha added more weight. It was one thousand pounds now. For a moment, she thought she wouldn't be able to get the bar over her head. Her arms started to ache, but she did it. "This is—this is—"

"I'd say we should add more weight," Ella said, "but there isn't any more space on the bar."

Aisha put the weights back, and they left the weight room to go home.

"Now at least you understand it a little better," Ella said outside the school.

"Thank you, Ella," Aisha said. She cleared her throat before looking up at Ella. "But why are you helping me?"

Ella chuckled a little. "I'm pretty sure that I'm as curious as you are about what you can do." She pointed a thumb at herself.

"Journalist," she said, and then added, "I'll see you tomorrow. Work on your pen skills. I saw your notes—pretty sloppy, Muscles." Ella started walking home.

Aisha shook her head, smiling. *Not a bad day*, she thought. She had this ability more or less under control, and not only that, what she could do was incredible. *Besides, Ella kept my secret. I know what I can do, and we finished an article!* she thought. *Take* that, *new life!*

At home, her father was finishing up dinner when she came in the door. She sat down immediately, and, feeling confident, picked up her fork. It didn't bend at all. She held it in her hand, smiling at it until her father said, "You planning on asking that fork to prom?"

Aisha felt her face turn red and began eating. "Uh, no. Just super hungry, I guess."

"You seem extra peppy today. Good day at school?" her dad asked.

"Yeah," she said. "The paper's good. The people I told you about are good." She nodded to herself. "I think things are going to be okay here."

He smiled. "Glad to hear it."

Aisha tried to help her dad clean up after dinner, but he shooed her away and told her to start on her homework instead. She plopped down on the couch with her backpack. While she was reading a passage in her history textbook, the pen she was twirling slipped between her fingers and rolled under the couch. She got down and tried to reach under it, but the pen had rolled farther than she could reach. She rolled her eyes as an idea popped into her head. *You can lift this couch, dummy.*

She raised the side of the couch way over her head with one hand and grabbed the pen with the other. The moment she lowered the couch back down, she realized her mistake. She turned to face her father, who had stopped wiping off a dish. He was staring at her with his mouth open.

7

Aisha stood up and faced her father, who still hadn't moved. Or closed his mouth yet.

"I, umm," she said, "I've been working out?"

Her dad dropped the dish in the sink. "Do you remember when the moving van got here? It took four guys bigger than I am to get that thing up here." He sat down at the kitchen table and stared at the floor.

"I don't know what happened, Dad," Aisha said. She came over to the table and sat across from him. "A couple days ago, I started breaking things without meaning to, and now—now I can do this, and I don't know why."

He didn't say anything. He closed his eyes and took a deep breath. Aisha knew he was counting to ten in his head. She stayed silent while he did it, but the silence made the ten seconds feel like a half hour. "Your alarm clock?" he finally said.

"I didn't knock it off the shelf. I just tried to turn it off."

"Your door knob?"

"I crushed it."

"The pens, pencils, and backpack?"

"My fault. I've gotten better though. I'm starting to get a better handle on it."

She explained about testing her strength at the junkyard and the school weight room. He nodded and went silent again. Aisha was practically shaking in anxiety—she couldn't tell what her father was thinking. She wanted him to assure her that everything would be all right, that he would help her keep the secret.

He had been motionless for so long that she jumped when he turned toward her and said, "Let's go." He got up from the table, grabbed his keys, and headed toward the front door.

"Go where?" she asked.

"Back to that junkyard."

It was close to dusk when they got there. In the distance, Aisha could see dark clouds rolling closer. A storm was coming in. Aisha led her dad to the same corner where the pieces of scrap she'd used for practice were still scattered around.

"So?" he said. "What can you do?"

"I don't know exactly," Aisha answered. "I know I can lift a lot though."

He nodded and pointed to a broken washing machine. "How about that?"

She walked over to it, bent down, and wrapped her arms around the appliance. She lifted it easily. After holding it for a moment, she put it down.

Her dad smiled and chuckled, shaking his head. His reaction made Aisha laugh a little too. "What about . . . that," he said, pointing to an old refrigerator. Aisha walked over and lifted it just as easily as the washing machine, although it was slightly heavier. Her dad laughed again. "Okay," he said, "let's get ambitious. See if you can lift that." He pointed to a rusted out sedan in the corner of the yard.

The thing was huge, and Aisha had to figure out how to lift it first. Eventually she decided to lift up the front to see if she could, then take it from there.

She stood between the headlights, grabbed the frame below the bumper, and lifted. It was easy enough. The back wheels were still on the ground, but she had gotten the front end up to her neck and was preparing to get it over her head when the thing started to break apart. There was a horrible sound of ripping and twisting metal, then a crash. Aisha was left holding the entire front of the car, engine and all, over her head. The seats and trunk in the back half had fallen back to the ground.

When she looked at her father, he was doubled over in laughter, slapping his leg. "That's amazing!" he shouted. "You can put it down now." She lightly tossed the front of the car to the side.

"I probably could have lifted the whole thing if it wasn't so rusty," she said.

"I'll bet you could," he replied through laughter, wiping his eye. "Come on, let's go home."

As they walked home, they heard thunder in the distance. It started raining just as they made it through the front entrance of their building.

"I don't want anyone to know I can do this," Aisha told her dad as they stepped into their living room.

He smiled at her. "If you don't want anyone to know, my lips are sealed."

"I'm sorry I didn't tell you right away. I just didn't know what was happening."

He put a hand on her shoulder. "I'm not sure I would have told me either. This is a lot to deal with. But you don't have to worry about dealing with it alone."

Aisha yawned. It had been another long day, and she still had some homework left to do.

"Hey, Dad?"

"Yeah?"

"I love you."

"I love you too. Now get started on your homework."

8

The storm that night was bad. Aisha woke up
three times because of thunder that sounded
more like a series of explosions. When she
got up for the day, the storm had passed and
the sun was out. Her dad made breakfast and
they chatted as usual. He never mentioned
the events of the previous night. Aisha
was grateful for that. Life could continue
as normal.

It was getting easier to keep from breaking
things. She even took her bike to school
and made it through the whole day without
breaking a writing utensil. Her notes were still
sloppy, but at least she could read them.

After her last class, she headed down to the newspaper office and found Ella, Ben, and Cal all huddled around a computer. "What's going on?" she asked.

"Two things," Ben said, turning around. "One: the biggest, oldest tree in Greenway Park got blown over in the storm last night. The city wants to haul it away, but a lot of people in the area want it replanted. Two, Ella still has a secret, but she—"

"Won't tell him," Ella finished.

"The third thing that's happened," Cal said, "is that I've gotten really annoyed with these two."

"That's not newsworthy," Ben said.

"And the tree is?" Aisha asked with a snort. "How old is this tree?"

"Almost three hundred years old," Cal answered. "It's a historical landmark. There's a plaque and everything."

"The problem," Ella said, "is that the city wants to cut it up and haul it away, but the people who want it replanted don't know how to get it back into its hole. They can tie it to a vehicle and drag it, but they can't get it upright again." She stared intently at Aisha. "They can't *lift* it."

"What are the odds that it would survive if they got it back where it's supposed to be?" Cal asked.

"Who knows? Maybe fifty-fifty," Ella said.

"No one will be able to get it back in the hole," Ben said confidently. "The city's going to trash it."

Aisha looked at the article they were writing. It said that unless someone with the means to move the massive tree stepped in, the city would in fact chop it up and haul it away. In the corner, there was a picture of the tree. Aisha recognized it from the park not far from her apartment. It was gigantic. She had learned in the gym that her strength did have limits. A thousand pounds had been a strain, and the tree definitely weighed much, much more than that. Her eyes went wide as she looked at Ella and shook her head.

With Ella doing the typing, the four of them finished the article and submitted it to

Mr. Westlake. He gave it the thumbs-up, and the group was free to leave for the day. Once they were out of the basement, Ella asked Aisha to hang back while Ben and Cal headed home.

"You should put the tree back," she said.

"No way," Aisha responded. "That thing's huge. I don't think I can lift it."

"Look, there's only one person in this town that even has a chance. You have to at least try."

Aisha crossed her arms. "Why do you care about some tree this much anyway?"

"I guess . . ." Ella started, looking down as she thought it over. "My family goes back generations in this town—apparently someone from my family was even there when the tree was planted. So, I don't know, it's like, a sentimental thing to us. Ben and I played around it all the time when we were little—lots of kids in town did."

Though she was still hesitant, Aisha felt her resolve weakening. Eventually she threw her hands up in the air and groaned. "All right, fine. I'll try. But I don't want someone to see me doing it."

"Then we'll go late at night," Ella said. "*Tonight.*"

Aisha reluctantly agreed, and the two agreed to meet at the tree at midnight.

It wasn't hard for Aisha to sneak out. Her dad was a heavy sleeper, and Greenway Park was only a few blocks away from their apartment building. When Aisha arrived, even in the dark, it was easy to find the tree. It was lying on its side, and Ella was sitting with her back up against the trunk scrolling through her phone. The tree was even larger than the photo had made it look, and the area around it was littered with sticks and branches that had snapped off when the top hit the ground. It must have been four or five stories tall.

No wonder the idea of replanting it was so tricky, Aisha thought. *A crane may not be able to lift it.*

"We just want it over there," Ella shouted, pointing at the huge hole the tree had left several yards away.

"Keep your voice down," Aisha said. "I don't want anyone to see." She looked down the trunk of the tree toward the top and felt the doubt creep back in. *This is impossible.* "I don't think I can do this."

Ella crossed her arms. "You could at least try."

Aisha dug her fingers into the bark of the trunk and tried to lift. It didn't move. She took a deep breath, got a firmer grip, and tried as hard as she could to raise it. She thought maybe it would roll since the trunk was so wide, and she wasn't even close to gripping the middle. It moved, but just barely, before Aisha had to let go. She stepped back, breathing hard from the effort.

"Well," Ella said, "it was worth a shot."

I can't lift it, Aisha thought. *But I'll bet I can drag it.* "I think I can do it."

"Really?"

Aisha walked toward the bottom of the tree where some roots were sticking out. She wrapped her left arm around the thickest one she could find near the center of the trunk. Then she pulled as hard as she could, attempting to drag the tree toward the hole.

It was working. Inch by inch, the tree was sliding, but Aisha wasn't sure she was going to make it. Her arms felt like they were tearing in half. Her calves and thighs burned, and she could feel her pulse throbbing in her forehead.

She was close to quitting when, finally, she reached the hole. Letting go and breathing heavily, she walked toward the top of the tree. *Almost done.* She grabbed one of the larger branches and started pushing it. The branch creaked and threatened to break, but the tree started slipping back into the hole and tilting slightly upward as it did. She got under the trunk and gave it one powerful push up, and the tree slammed back into place with a huge *THUD*.

Aisha, completely exhausted, collapsed and rolled onto her back in the dirt. She was seeing stars, and her whole body felt like it was melting.

She was just getting control of her breath back when Ella said, "Nice job!" She jogged over to stand above Aisha. "Bad news: I don't think the tree's going to make it. Its whole side got crushed when it fell over. It's basically just half a tree now. We should have let the city cut it up."

Aisha groaned, throwing an arm over her eyes. "Great."

9

"Hey." Aisha looked up from her lunch to see Ella sliding into the seat next to her with her own lunch tray.

"I had study hall second period, so I wrote this." She handed Aisha a piece of paper. "I'll turn it in to Mr. Westlake after school, and it should run in the next issue," Ella explained. "Also, I had been assuming you had a different lunch period than us. Have you been eating alone in this corner the whole time?"

Aisha read the headline: HISTORIC TREE REPLANTED. She couldn't hold the question in. "You didn't—"

"All I know," Ella said, "is that *someone* put the tree back." She turned over her shoulder and waved. Aisha glanced behind her to see Ben and Cal heading over with lunch bags in hand.

"So *this* is where you've been sitting every day," Cal said as he dropped into the chair across from her.

Aisha flushed—she had been eating alone every day at lunch since she'd moved to Bloomington. She hadn't been expecting the others to come find her, but it was nice to have people to sit with.

She felt relieved when no one said anything else about it and moved on with the conversation. Ella showed the boys her article about the tree.

"Maybe someone used a pickup truck after all," Ben guessed.

"Doubt it," Cal said. "They tried that yesterday when they found it, remember? All they could do was drag it." He peered closer at the article. Aisha glanced nervously at Ella, who just sipped at her lemonade. "It would have been hard to move in a week, much less a single night."

"Well," Aisha said quickly, "someone pulled it off." Before the boys could take any more guesses, she cleared her throat and said, "Hey, are there good pizza places in Bloomington? I haven't had pizza since I got here."

"Oh!" Ben shouted. "There's—"

"Don't say Lenny's," Ella cut him off.

"Lenny's!" Ben finished anyway.

"Don't go to Lenny's," Cal and Ella said in unison.

"Hmm," Aisha teasingly pretended to think it over. "Should we try Lenny's?" Cal and Ella groaned, while Ben threw up a fist in a cheer. Aisha just laughed.

***

The next two weeks were easy. Aisha was getting a better and better hold on her ability. Even the quality of her notes improved. She was able to use the computer in the paper's office without breaking the keyboard.

Her father found a bigger apartment for them to move into. When they'd come to Bloomington, they had hired a moving company. This time, Aisha's dad rented a truck. Her dad moved boxes, she moved furniture. They did it late at night, so no one would see. The next night, he ordered pizza from anywhere but Lenny's.

Not only had her strength come in handy during the move, but Ella had pushed her to use it to do some good around the school. Aisha would secretly fix something, and Ella would write about it. The headlines appeared every few days.

BENT FLAG POLE MYSTERIOUSLY STRAIGHTENED

BROKEN BLEACHERS NOW PROPPED UP BY I-BEAM

She wasn't perfect. There were also some headlines detailing her mistakes.

BRAND-NEW WATER FOUNTAIN COLLAPSES

CAFETERIA TABLE SNAPPED IN HALF

BIG HOLE IN GYMNASIUM WALL: STUDENTS DEBATE CAUSE

Ella wrote those stories too. "News is news," she said with a shrug one day at the office.

"You're not even in the school news group," Aisha replied. "You're supposed to be covering events out in the community."

"When I see a story, I write a story. It's my duty to our readers."

Aisha just rolled her eyes. Truth be told, the negative stories didn't bother her much. They never made any mention of her name or pointed the finger at anyone for the damage. Sometimes she thought that Ella was writing them just to tease her. As long as she kept the secret, Aisha didn't mind.

She got into a comfortable groove in her new home. She was doing well in all her classes. Every day, she had friends to eat with at lunch, and after school, she'd go to the paper's office to work on whatever article they had to write.

"We should probably mention something about local businesses," Ella said. "You know, remind people that it's good to support restaurants that are only in Bloomington."

"Good idea," Aisha said. They were covering a story about a burger place that was opening soon, but it was part of a chain and could pose a threat to the local burger joints. Ella was talking over her shoulder while Aisha typed.

"You two still working on that?" Cal asked, stepping up behind them. The room was deserted—the rest of the students had already left, and Mr. Westlake had run off to grab something from the main office.

"We're almost done," Ella responded.

"Speaking of burgers," Cal said, "want to go grab one? I'm starving."

"That sounds great," Aisha said, typing up a final sentence. "Where's Ben?"

"Right here." He was leaning behind a desk shoving books into his bag. "I'll get a burger."

Aisha was just about to print the article when she felt a rumbling, like the table was vibrating.

It got steadily stronger. All four of them noticed it now. They looked in every direction to find its source, but couldn't see anything out of the ordinary.

The computer monitor flickered and went dead along with the lights in the room. The rumbling was getting violent now. Old binders, notebooks, and computer monitors toppled off desks and shelves. After a few seconds of darkness, the emergency lights flickered on.

There was a constant rumble, like a train was driving right over them.

Suddenly, there was a tremendous *CRACK* that sounded like someone just snapped a house in half, and Aisha felt the whole room shift and tilt. She fell out of her chair and felt a pile of books fall on top of her. Something was breaking in the ceiling above her. It sounded like someone was snapping wood planks. The shaking became so intense that she couldn't even see straight.

Then the shaking subsided and the rumbling stopped. The whole event could have lasted one minute or five. Aisha wasn't sure. And now the rumbling had been replaced by another sound—rushing water. When the world finally stood still, the office was dark, only illuminated by the few emergency lights, and it took her eyes a moment to adjust. Everything was in disarray. Desks had shifted during the rumbling and were scattered all over the room. And then Aisha saw the source of the new noise. A water main had broken. The pipe was angled toward the floor and was gushing water into the room.

"Ben?" Ella shouted over the rushing sound of the water. "Cal? Aisha?"

"I'm here!" It was Cal, splashing as he crawled out from beneath a desk he had hidden under. Aisha felt a small wave wash over her shoes. The water was coming in so fast that in just the few moments it took to realize what was happening, it was already up to Aisha's ankles.

A large cabinet opened in the corner of the room to Aisha's right. It was Ben. "Was that an earthquake?"

"I think so!" Ella shouted. They started shuffling toward one another, which was extra difficult due to the way the floor had started shifting into the ground.

Cal was by the door, propping himself against the wall. The door frame had bent, locking it in place. He pulled and pulled, but it wouldn't open. He turned around. "We're trapped!"

10

The water was already up to their knees. Time was running out. While Ben and Cal desperately tried to open the door, Ella looked expectantly at Aisha.

"The door won't budge!" Ben shouted.

Aisha was still trying to process what was happening.

"Maybe we can get out through that vent," Call suggested, pointing to a vent that was far too high for any of them to reach.

"What are you waiting for?" Ella shouted at Aisha. "Get us out of here!"

Aisha looked at Cal and Ben, both still shifting around in the water and desperately trying to find an alternative way out of the room. *I don't have a choice*, she thought. *If we stay here, we die.* She waded through the water, now waist-high, to the jammed door. She gripped the handle tightly and yanked. *CRACK*. The door didn't just pop open—it came straight off its hinges.

She tossed the door to the side and caught a quick glimpse of Cal and Ben, both frozen in place, with shocked looks on their faces.

"Let's go!" she shouted at them. No time to explain.

The hallway outside the office was filled with dust, smoke, and water. There was another broken pipe and the hallway was flooding too. It was so disorienting that Aisha couldn't remember which way led to the stairs. She turned to the right but felt a hand on her shoulder. It was Cal.

"There's an emergency stairwell down this hall!" he shouted, pointing to the left.

They didn't make it very far before they had to stop. A massive chunk of concrete—a piece of the floor above them—was blocking their path.

"We have to go the other way," Cal said.

"No," Aisha said. "I can clear a way through." She put her right elbow against the middle of the concrete slab like a chisel and made a fist. With her left hand, she pounded on her fist, and a crack shot up and down the concrete. Behind her, she heard Ben say, "How—" The sound of her hitting the concrete again cut him off. She repeated the process until the giant piece crumbled into a pile of rubble. Aisha crawled over the pile first, and then helped the others over.

It was hard to see. The emergency lighting in the building only did so much. There was so much dust and smoke from whatever had happened that everything seemed blurry and Aisha could only see a couple of feet in front of her.

The water had gotten so high it was up to Aisha's chest. She was half walking and half swimming and they couldn't even see the exit yet. Cal shouted directions from the back of the line, occasionally spitting out water as he did so.

They rounded corner after corner. Aisha couldn't understand how Cal seemed to know his way around this mess—the hallways were unrecognizable to her. They hadn't gone far, but she would have had trouble just navigating back to the office.

"It's just around this corner," Cal shouted.

Aisha was swimming now, easily able to touch the ceiling, and the water was still rising quickly. She guessed they had about a minute before the hallway was completely underwater.

They turned a corner, and Aisha could see the red illuminated exit sign just barely peeking over the water line.

"Go, go, go!" Ella shouted.

All four of them swam as fast as they could toward the exit, but the water was rising too quickly. Aisha felt her head bump against the ceiling, and they were still about fifty feet from the door.

Aisha's ability to lift impossible weights wasn't helping with the strain of having to swim this hard. Her arms and legs ached, but she had to keep going. They had to swim the last thirty feet completely under water. When they finally reached the door, Aisha felt along the wall for the push bar that would open the exit. She pushed as hard as she could. The door opened, and the water surged forward, taking Aisha and her friends with it.

Aisha's head popped out of the water. Gasping for breath, she glanced around. They were in a concrete nook at the bottom of a fire escape stairwell. She grabbed the first arm she found—Ben's—and pulled him up until his head appeared. Ella and Cal's heads appeared just a moment later.

The water level had lowered a bit as it spread out throughout the basement, but it still lapped at several stairs at the bottom of the stairwell. Sopping wet, the group climbed the stairs up to ground level. They burst out the door, coming out on a side of the school. Aisha could hear sirens and see flickers of red and blue lights from around the corner, where the parking lot was. They ran toward the flashing lights.

Emergency vehicles and officers filled the parking lot. Behind them stood several other students and teachers who'd still been in the building when the earthquake hit. An EMT rushed toward Aisha and her friends as they trudged across the parking lot.

"Are you kids all right?" she asked, looking them all over. They were each covered in a brownish gray coating, probably from the dirty water and all the dust from the rubble. That was hardly a problem right now though. Out of breath, all they could do was nod. "Come over here, we'll get you each looked at." She led them over to where the ambulances were gathered.

As she waited to be looked over, Aisha turned around to face the school. Two-thirds of it was gone, sunken into the ground, where a massive hole had opened up. What was left standing was teetering, threatening to fall. Looking at it, Aisha was shocked she and her friends had survived at all. They were lucky the newspaper office was under the part of the school that was still standing. If it hadn't been, they could have been crushed instantly.

"One of the firefighters said it's a sinkhole," the EMT explained. "The quake wasn't very severe, but it was enough to open that up."

Aisha checked behind her to make sure her friends were still okay. Then her stomach dropped. *They all know*, she realized. *They've seen what I can do.* They were standing next to a different ambulance a few parking spaces away. Aisha watched as they whispered to one another and pointed at her.

Her secret was blown.

11

"They're still in there!"

Aisha was pulled from her worried thoughts as she turned to see a student behind her shouting and pointing to the corner room of the third floor. Just as he said it, the remaining portion of the building shifted slightly toward the hole. It was going to fall in. It was only a matter of time.

"Who?" a firefighter asked.

"My friends," the boy said. "We were in our classroom, practicing for debate. I was on the first floor getting something from my locker, so I got out really fast. But I can't find them anywhere—they must still be in there!"

"Don't worry," the firefighter said. "We'll figure something out." He returned to a group of other emergency responders, and Aisha could see the looks of concern on their faces.

I could get them out, Aisha thought. She took another look at her friends. They had stopped whispering and were all staring directly at her. *Sorry, guys*, she thought. *Still don't have time to explain.*

She ran around the crowd of onlookers and back to the stairwell where she and her friends had escaped. The firefighters never noticed her.

The stairs were tilted at an angle, and she could feel them shifting slightly with every step she took. She was going up to the third floor as fast as she could, but the tilt made her feel nauseous. She pushed through it and reached the entrance.

Normally, this hallway would run the entire length of the school, but now, it only went for about thirty yards before there was an open-air drop off down into the sinkhole.

Aisha paused at the classroom door immediately to her left. Through it, Aisha could hear muffled banging and calls for help coming from inside the room. She yanked the knob, but somehow the door was stuck shut. She pulled hard, and it snapped open, splintering part of the frame.

Four students inside were inside. For a second, they just stared at Aisha, clearly confused how the door had opened so easily for her.

"Come on!" she shouted at them.

Just as she said it, the building lurched, rumbled, and tilted again. Aisha heard a sound like a bunch of pipes banging together and turned to see the fire escape staircase fall out of sight.

She turned left, headed away from the emergency exit, glancing behind to make sure the students were following.

The school had two primary staircases, one on each side of the building. The one on this side of the school was just a few yards ahead. Aisha and the others made it to the stairs, but part of the roof had collapsed onto them.

Aisha stopped in her tracks. There was far too much debris to moves piece by piece, but at the bottom she spotted the straight edge of a steel plate. Using all the strength she could muster, she lifted it—along with all the debris on top—high enough for the four students to crawl underneath. They made it through a hole where a railing should be and hopped down to the next flight of stairs. Some of them gave her an amazed look as they moved past her.

They couldn't go all the way to the bottom. The staircase below the second floor landing had crumbled, and a fire was burning below. There was another rumbling, and the building violently shook. One of the students, with tears running down her cheeks, turned to Aisha and yelled, "We're not going to make it!"

"This way!" Aisha shouted to the group. They ran to the fire escape door. She kicked it open, snapping the latch on the side. Below the ledge, the staircase had collapsed into a heap of jagged metal on concrete. It would only be a one-story fall, but if they jumped, it was likely they'd all seriously injure themselves.

Aisha thought of the grassy lawn at the back of the school. She led the students through a door to the teachers' lounge, where the windows faced the rear of the building. She grabbed a chair and whipped it, one-handed, through a window. The glass shattered, and Aisha and the others ran to the exit she'd just created.

It was a significant drop, but it would definitely be better than hanging around in the ruins of the school waiting for it to collapse on them. The building tipped more, threatening to fall over at any moment.

She stepped closer to the window and noticed the shards of glass scattered everywhere. "You," she said, pointing to a boy behind her wearing a hoodie, "give me your sweatshirt."

He quickly pulled it over his head and tossed it to her. Aisha bunched it up and used it to wipe away the remaining pieces of glass on the windowsill as best she could.

Then, one at a time, Aisha held the students' arms as they climbed out the window and dangled from it. When they were as low as they could get, she let go, and they dropped down onto the grass. Once all four were out, Aisha herself climbed out, lowering herself as much as she could until she was just gripping the window ledge. She let herself fall. She hit the ground with a thud and quickly picked herself up.

The four students formed a semi-circle around her, mouths open and eyes wide. She wanted to hide from their stares. She wanted to erase their memories, but all she could do was shout, "Get away from the building!"

They scattered, running toward the emergency responders.

The ground began to rumble again. For a second, she thought another earthquake was happening, but that wasn't the cause. The rest of the school was coming down. Aisha raced back toward the parking lot. Just as she made it to the row of ambulances, the last part of the building fell into the sinkhole with a tremendous crash.

Her heart was pounding so heavily in her

chest she felt like it might burst. Aisha leaned forward, resting her hands on her knees, as she struggled to catch her breath. She couldn't believe what had just happened. Running back into the school had been dangerous— and maybe not the wisest decision she'd ever made—but she'd saved those kids. And she made it out alive.

Aisha looked for her friends, but she couldn't see them anywhere. Fear and worry twisted in the pit of her stomach. *They're probably off telling everyone what they saw.* Ella hadn't treated her any differently, but she didn't trust the rest of Bloomington to be as kind. *Once the news gets out, I'll be the freakish strong girl. I'll never have a friend again.* As an EMT led her away from the rubble, she couldn't help tears gathering in her eyes.

12

It took a while for people to get through the mess of traffic in the streets, but eventually everyone's parents and family members had arrived to pick them up from the school. Aisha's dad was one of the last to make it there, and she didn't know if she'd ever been more relieved to see him in her life.

At home, Aisha immediately took a shower. The grime from the dust and the dirty water took forever to wash off. Once she was cleaned up and dressed again, she headed into the kitchen. Her dad was sitting at the table. She sat down across from him. She could tell he was waiting for her to explain what had happened, and she was admittedly a little nervous to tell him about running back into the school. He was shocked and shaken while she told the story, but he didn't seem angry. He didn't say anything for a long moment.

"A hard day's work deserves a something good to eat," he said eventually, getting up and walking toward the refrigerator. He slid a pint of ice cream and a spoon across the table to her as he sat back down. "You can eat healthy some other day."

"Thanks," she said, dipping the spoon into the dessert. After a moment of eating in silence, she asked, "So, you're not mad at me?"

Her dad leaned back in his chair, rubbing his hand over his face. "What you did was risky, and I can't say that I would have let you run in there if I'd been with you. But I get why you did it. The firefighters might not have been able to get to those kids in time. They're safe because of you. That's something to be proud of."

"No one is ever going to treat me like a normal person ever again."

"You did what you thought was right."

Aisha gave a sad smile back to him. "I just wish I could have hidden my identity or something."

He chuckled. "We can get you a costume. I'm thinking something in red. How do you feel about capes?"

Even though she was mentally, physically, and emotionally exhausted, Aisha chuckled a little too.

They ate the rest of the ice cream in silence, sliding it back and forth across the table between them. When it was gone, Aisha thought about texting Ella, but she didn't want to find out that her ability had been exposed, not right now. Instead she went to bed early. As soon as she closed her eyes she fell into a deep sleep.

***

School was canceled for a week. After that, most of the classes temporarily relocated to extra rooms at the middle school, and the rest were at the rec center just across the street.

Aisha thought about texting her friends every day, but she could never work up the nerve. She was too terrified of what they would say to her, what they thought of her now.

She confided her worries to her dad. "There's nothing in the local news about you. Maybe your friends kept quiet," he said.

"Or maybe they just want the school paper to have the story first," she replied.

"I think you should give your friends a little more credit."

The Saturday before school was supposed to start up again, Aisha got an email from Mr. Westlake. There would be a meeting for the school paper that night at the public library. He wanted to get an issue of the paper ready before Monday so students could read it between classes.

The last line of the email made Aisha lose all hope of maintaining a normal life. It read: "The local news group has already gotten in touch with me, and they have an absolutely fascinating article about the sinkhole, a story even the *Bloomington Press* doesn't know about."

It has to be me, Aisha thought, reading the line over and over again. *What else could it be?*

She showed the message to her dad. She saw his face fall after he was done reading it, but he put a hand on her shoulder and said, "Go to the meeting. We could be wrong."

Aisha walked slowly to the library when it was time. She could lift a car over her head, but today she felt like even heavier weights were attached to each of her limbs.

That thought made her stop. She could lift a car over her head. Regardless of what anyone else thought about that, she knew it was an incredible ability. Hiding from everyone wouldn't make her life easier or better. She should be proud of what she could do, even if others couldn't accept her for it.

When she got to the library, she paused before heading inside. She felt her confidence suddenly disappear. *I could just go home*, she thought. *I could just tell Dad I can't face them.* But then she remembered what her dad had said—and what she'd said to herself—and trudged through the doors.

Inside, Mr. Westlake was sitting at one of the tables. Aisha didn't want to talk to him. The only people she cared about speaking to right now were the ones in her group.

Cal, Ella, and Ben were huddled over a computer in the corner. She took a deep breath, prepared for the worst, and walked over to them.

Cal was at the keyboard. "I think we should leave that part out," he said to Ben and Ella.

"People are going think it's weird if there's no description at all," Ben said. "They obviously saw her."

"Yeah, but we can just—oh, hey, Muscles," Cal said when he saw Aisha standing behind them. "We're just putting the finishing touches on our sinkhole article."

"What did you write?" Aisha was barely able to choke out the words, and she couldn't bring herself to look over them and read what was on the computer.

Ella spun around in a chair with a grin. "We got exclusive interviews with four students who say they were rescued by a girl who was able to move debris that no human should be able to lift." She pointed to the screen. "Apparently this girl was about your height, probably with hair that's the same color and length as yours."

"Yeah," Cal said, "but we should leave that part out of it. With all the dust and soot and stuff, how could they reliably tell what hair color she had?"

"So . . ." Aisha wasn't sure what she wanted to ask.

"Unfortunately," Ella continued talking as if Aisha hadn't said anything, "the four students couldn't identify the person who rescued them because—"

"She was so covered in dust from the collapse, they didn't recognize her," Ben finished the sentence.

"We may never know who it was," Cal said with a smile. "On a *completely* unrelated note, you may want to consider getting a haircut."

Aisha couldn't help but smile, and she felt some tears well up in her eyes. Her dad had been right. She really hadn't given her friends enough credit. The weight she had felt walking into the library immediately evaporated. She grabbed Cal and Ben and pushed them toward Ella, forcing them all into a group hug.

"I'm glad you like the article," Ella said, laughing. She turned to Ben. "Do you want to tell her?"

Ben smiled. He leaned down and grabbed a box from underneath the desk. "We got you something. Think of it as a welcome to Bloomington gift and our way of saying we're happy you're here."

Aisha was just about to open the box when all three of them lunged forward and stopped her. "You may not want to do that here," Ella said.

They finished the article and turned it in to Mr. Westlake. "Great job," he said. "The *BHS Herald* is the only paper in town with this story!"

On their way out of the library, the four friends made plans to see a movie the next day and then parted ways. Aisha practically danced home carrying her gift.

Back at her apartment, she finally opened the box. Under some tissue paper, there was a weight-lifting belt spray painted gold with a circular plaque on the center. It read:

FOR OUR HERO, THE STRONGEST
PERSON IN BLOOMINGTON

THREE MONTHS LATER

LOCAL HERO SAVES FAMILY OF FIVE

Last night's tornado did a great deal of damage, but one family was saved by an anonymous stranger. Their car had been flipped over by the wind and blown up against a tree. Before they were able to get out, another tree was lodged against the car, trapping the family inside. They report that a girl wearing a mask pulled the tree aside and ripped off the door of their vehicle so they were able to crawl to safety.

Patricia Delano, the mother trapped in the car, said, "She didn't say anything and wouldn't tell us who she was. After she helped us, she just ran off." The Delano family has asked the *BHS Herald* to pass on their sincerest gratitude to the anonymous stranger.

HAVING A SUPERPOWER IS NOT AS EASY
AS THE COMIC BOOKS MAKE IT SEEM.

CHECK OUT ALL OF THE TITLES IN THE

SERIES

MIND OVER MATTER	STRETCHED TOO THIN
NOW YOU SEE ME	STRONGHOLD
PICKING UP SPEED	TAKE TO THE SKIES

WHAT WOULD YOU DO IF YOU WOKE UP IN A
VIDEO GAME?

CHECK OUT ALL OF THE TITLES IN THE

LEVEL UP

SERIES

DAY OF DISASTER

AFTERSHOCK

BACKFIRE

BLACK BLIZZARD

DEEP FREEZE

VORTEX

WALL OF WATER

Would you survive?

ABOUT THE AUTHOR

R. T. Martin lives in St. Paul, Minnesota. When he is not drinking coffee or writing, he is busy thinking about drinking coffee and writing.